DOORMAT

DOORMAT

Delacorte Press

a novel by
KELLY McWILLIAMS

Published by
Delacorte Press
an imprint of
Random House Children's Books
a division of Random House, Inc.
New York

Visit us on the Web! www.randomhouse.com/teens
Educators and librarians, for a variety of teaching tools, visit us at
www.randomhouse.com/teachers

Library of Congress Cataloging-in-Publication Data
McWilliams, Kelly.
Doormat : a novel / by Kelly McWilliams.
p. cm.
Summary: Fourteen-year-old Jaime has always been a doormat, but her
diary reveals how getting the lead in a school play, finding her first
boyfriend, discovering her dream, and helping her best friend cope with
being pregnant transform her life.
ISBN 0-385-73168-X (trade) – ISBN 0-385-90204-2 (GLB)
[1. Pregnancy–Fiction. 2. Theater–Fiction. 3. Best friends–Fiction.
4. Friendship–Fiction. 5. California–Fiction. 6. Diaries–Fiction.]
I. Title.

PZ7.M47885Do 2004
[Fic]–dc22
2003019675

The text of this book is set in 11.5-point Baskerville BE.

Book design by Angela Carlino

Printed in the United States of America

September 2004

10 9 8 7 6 5 4 3 2 1

BVG

To Girl Scout
Troop 881
and to
the Kaufmans

DOORMAT

MODEL

My best friend thinks she's pregnant.

Personally, I think Melissa's wrong, but it's not my body. Teen pregnancy is so melodramatic: lonely, living off the streets and welfare, dragging your baby from city to city and everywhere but on your acid trips. No, fourteen-year-olds don't get pregnant anywhere except in the newspaper and on TV. I mean, what would Aunt Sheila say?

"Oh, drama," she'd sigh, and flip her curly hair.

So why am I so worried about this? Because worry is contagious, I guess. Melissa is having a heart attack about it:

"What should I do, Jaime? Should I ask my mother? Will she *hate* me?"

Or worse: "What about my modeling career?"

And then she'll cry, and the contagion has spread.

Now, here's the truth about Melissa's modeling career—she doesn't have one, and though I love her dearly, I doubt she ever will. And that's not to say she's not beautiful; who am I to talk? It's her attitude that's the problem. She expects life on a silver platter with oysters and an Amex, and her god-awful parents hate the very idea of her doing anything so superficial and are working with all their authoritative might to stop that career before it begins. I remember discussing this with her over the summer in depth:

"I want to be a model," she said.

"Okay. But why?"

"Because I want to be beautiful!"

"Don't you think there's more to life than that?" Even to me it sounded half-baked. I knew Melissa wouldn't go for it.

"Who are you, Gandhi? Give me a break! I want to be a model. Who says there even has to *be* a reason? The point is I need your help because my parents aren't going for it."

"What do you mean, not going for it?"

"Oh, you know my mother."

Translation—they'd be shopping at Target for new china any day now, and they'd need the carpets professionally cleaned.

Melissa is under the impression that she hates her mother. She tends to get stuck in a swamp of self-pity at the mention of the M-word, and that makes for uncomfortable silences. I don't think I hate my mother, myself. But I can't be completely sure; I haven't really thought about it since sometime around the fourth grade.

"Well, what do you think I can do about it?" I asked.

"Get me engagements! Jobs!" she said. Shouted, if you want to know the truth.

"Jobs?"

"Yeah, you know, photo shoots at clothing stores and places, obviously. You can be my agent! Agents get half the money, you know. And we could go all sorts of places together and meet all sorts of famous people. . . ."

"Melissa . . ."

"Just ask around at the malls and stuff, okay?"

"Whatever."

Okay, let me start from the very beginning. I was sitting alone in the cafeteria at lunchtime Friday, minding my own business. Mostly I was pretending to be invisible, because, believe it or not, it's not *easy* to sit alone in the hostile environment of a school cafeteria. In spite of my best efforts to make it look like I was waiting for someone (foot on chair, checking my watch periodically) and thus increase my chances for survival, I could tell that no one was quite buying it.

Yeah, sure, their eyebrows said.

If there's one thing I hate, it's sassy eyebrows.

To top it all off, I'd been disturbed all day because of an unsettling event that occurred during second period. We filled out one of those career planning sheets in health class, but it wasn't the usual What's Your Favorite Subject type survey. Instead, I found myself answering questions like "What are you passionate about?" "What do you love?" "What is your most powerful dream?" What disturbed me was the number of questions that I had to leave blank.

Before I could think on it too heavily, however, Melissa ambled in at the back of the cafeteria food line. She looked over the serving counter doubtfully, kind of sniffed at it, and to my relief got out of line and walked straight over to me without stopping to pick up the apparently unsatisfactory chicken nuggets.

"Finally!" I said when she sat down. "What took you?"

"Nothing," she said absently.

I rolled my eyes. She wanted me to ask. I ate in silence for a minute, deciding whether or not to play along with her.

"So what's *wrong*?" I finally asked. Don't say I never do anything for her.

"Do I look fat to you?" she asked.

"No."

"Not just a little?"

"No."

"What about my cheeks? Are they puffy?"

"No."

4

"My legs?"

"No."

"You're sure?"

"Yes."

"Positive?"

"Yes!"

"Have I been eating more lately?"

"Melissa, what is it?"

Pause.

"I think I'm pregnant. Can you help me?"

So that's the story. Girl tells best friend she's pregnant. Best friend saves the world.

Under normal circumstances, I would simply notify the nearest adult as quickly as possible and let him or her handle it. Unfortunately, Melissa's last words have been stuck in my brain for the past six hours of my life, like a sappy song you hear on the radio.

"Can you help me?"

Why me? What can I do? I'm fourteen years old, for Christ's sakes! I don't know or care what I'm passionate about, I don't have any dreams, and I sure as hell don't know what to do about a baby.

After school, it took all my willpower to pick up the phone and dial her number.

I get the answering machine. I hang up.

COW

I finally reach Melissa Saturday afternoon, and her dramatic suspicions have only grown since Friday's lunch–her period is definitely late.

"So?" I say. "Didn't you listen in health class? Mine is too."

"Yeah, but when was the last time you had sex?" She sounds really nasty and bitter, and though I know better, I take offense at her words. I haven't had a boyfriend in two years. I've only been kissed once–at ten, by my next-door neighbor. I think everybody has been kissed at ten by their next-door neighbor. And I have acne like you wouldn't believe (oh, drama!). Confessions of your average fourteen-year-old.

I sidestep around her insinuations. "Who?" I ask, and that one word says it all.

Pause.

"I can't tell you," she says.

"Why not?" I ask indignantly. I've been her best friend too long for this.

"Be . . . cause," she mumbles.

I sigh, annoyed, and ask, "So did you use protection?"

Silence. Then—

"Not really."

"What's that supposed to mean?"

"It means not really!"

"Okay, okay, don't have a cow." I know it's wrong the second I say it.

"I *won't* have a cow, but I *might* have a baby!"

Melissa is nothing if not quick on the uptake.

Quiet again.

"So should I take that as a no?"

"Jaime! It doesn't matter! What am I going to do?" It sounds like Melissa is about to cry. I hate that.

"We don't know you're pregnant yet," I say quickly. That's me: rational as anything. "We need to get one of those tests. Like you see on TV."

"Right, so where am *I* going to get one of those tests? At Neiman Marcus?"

Dramatic tears to cutting sarcasm. "Um, why don't you just try Walgreens?"

"Oh, sure, and what will I tell my mother? 'Mom, I need to go to Walgreens . . . alone, please. No, nothing's wrong, I just need to buy a pregnancy test!' "

At this point I know that Melissa is just being stupid for the hell of it. If she couldn't get out of the house to go to Walgreens, how did she get out to get herself pregnant?

Exasperated, I say, "Fine. Calm down." And hang up.

Cows will fall from the sky before I go to Walgreens and get that pregnancy kit for her. She can get it herself.

●

I'm no longer so sure Melissa is imagining her pregnancy. And what does that mean? Baby showers? Abortion money? Stealthy trips to Planned Parenthood? Am I forgetting anything?

OASIS

(MONOLOGUE)

Okay, you have to understand something about me. I live in nowhere, California. As in *nowhere*. But while it's almost certainly nowhere to you, it's also just as certainly somewhere to me, because I've lived here for about as long as I can remember.

Where I live, the ground is parched like it's thirsty. You can't farm it, you can't dig in it, and it doesn't make any difference whether you water it or not. So someone somewhere in New York decided that they might as well sell it as real estate. And then someone somewhere in California decided that they might as well buy it, and build on it, and call the development the Oasis.

We bought a house in the Oasis shortly after I was born, and it didn't really matter which one we bought, either, because all the houses look exactly the same. They're all small, painted the color of rotten fruit, and they all have white mailboxes and a matching fence. Have I mentioned the community pool yet? That's my favorite part of the whole situation. While the houses are only slightly less drab than the landscape (for which the best thing that can be said is that it's flat and dry), our pool sparkles and glimmers enough to make up for an entire community of plainness. Maybe it's because of this that no one really swims in it. But when relatives come to town, the residents of the Oasis like to show it off a little, saying things like: "And if the heat starts to get to you, you can always go down to the club and have a dip in the pool."

I think they must have named our development the Oasis with the pool in mind, rather than the housing.

The school bus comes to our development on week-days, and on weekends a Greyhound stops at the bus station. I've never seen anyone from our community take the Greyhound, but it stops all the same, and everyone looks at it, and wonders what it would be like to hop on it one day with a knapsack and a ticket to New Mexico, or maybe Nevada. Outside the development is my school, and slightly past that is the city. The city sort of sneaks up on people if it's their first time seeing it. You'll be driving down the freeway from my house, admiring the wasteland to either side, and just when it looks like the pavement is going to stretch on forever and ever, an exit appears that shunts you promptly into light-exploding-noise-screaming-mind-boggling-magazine-selling-for-rent-only city.

It's a small city when compared to the cities in the rest of the world. Even just when compared to other cities in California. It's got supermarkets, bookstores, pizza places, porn places, and all the rest, but only in small doses. It threw my dad for a loop when we first came to this part of California. Originally he was from Chicago, so of course the size of the city was a shock to him. But what really got him about our city was the amount of time it takes to get to anywhere important or meaningful from where we live. We're talking four hours to Los Angeles, more to San Francisco, and three just to get to Disneyland. But I have to say that he made the best of it. He always said he liked how quiet it was, especially in the mornings, and he liked our house and our neighbors.

Mom, on the other hand, never shared his attitude toward our city. She called it the boonies, but always as a joke, you know? Because she seemed to think that this town was just a pit stop where she and Dad could get the money to start a new life somewhere else. Somewhere with a university where she could get a degree. The point is that she always treated our home like it was some sort of limbo.

Unfortunately for Mom, she was wrong. This place is hell. Dad left, and she lost her savings, and we took out a mortgage on our house.

I think the mortgage is what finally made it eternal.

But for me, I don't think this place is so bad. I have an iguana—his name is Jake—and we used to have some goldfish. I also have the most perfect room. It's a loft, with just enough space for a bed and desk. It's shaped like a triangle, so you can only stand up straight in the very middle of it. There's also plenty of light all the time, because it has these two huge windows like eyes without lids.

My mom hates my room. Claustrophobia, you know. But it's just as well for me, because I don't need her nosing around in there anyhow. And she scares the hell out of Jake.

WALGREENS

I don't remember my best friend ever being a wimp.

Coward.

Sucker.

But apparently she is, because not only did she fail to find a way to get the pregnancy test, she sent *me* to do it for her.

Remember what I said about cows falling from the sky before I went to Walgreens for Melissa? Yeah, well, what can I say? The Weather Channel just got a lot more interesting.

Of course, now I'm not sure who's more of a sucker. But I'm a sucker by nature, and always have been—in fact, I've been like this for so long that I'm practically a brand name. If you need lunch money, come to Jaime and you might even get her milk. If you want someone to scapegoat, look, there's Jaime over there! But you really know you're in trouble when your best friend starts exploiting you.

But for all that I'm a pitiful little muddy-foot door-mat, at least I'm a resourceful one—I called a taxi from my house, the yellow brick road to Walgreens.

In retrospect, the whole experience of purchasing that ugly little strip of paper was kind of like riding a roller coaster: In line, you feel just fine. You feel some butterflies in your stomach, maybe, but nothing major. Except then you get locked inside the car, and you have these moments of panic, like, "Quick! Get me out of here! I can't do it!" Or that's what I'm like anyway. I have a feeling Melissa says things more along the lines of "Wait, I have to go to the bathroom." Sure. Anyway, the taxi bit was fine. But then I ended up at the pharma-ceutical counter at Walgreens, face to face with a living, breathing employee. I walked toward the counter. Then I walked right out of the store.

The lady at the counter was a *man*! How could Melissa expect me to do this? I'd look just as pregnant as she is! How did I get pulled into this? Muddy feet, dog poo, and grass brought in from the rain, I thought. That's the kind of doormat I am.

But I walked back in and didn't look at anything un-til I reached pharmaceuticals. Then I hovered about for

14

a little while, debating in my head, while pretending to read a tabloid I wasn't even seeing:

You don't know this man. You'll be in and out in no time.
What if he calls my mother?
Can he do that? Would he do that?
Well, no, but he's a complete stranger.
So who cares what he thinks anyway?

I grabbed the little box (ugly little thing) and dragged my feet up to the counter–(ten dollars, please)–ignoring the harsh fluorescents laughing down my neck.

The man didn't even look up, but I saw his little smile as he bagged it. Or maybe that was just my imagination. Or maybe he was just having a really good day and was feeling especially friendly. The lights glared at me as I left, blinding me momentarily. They were saying, It wasn't supposed to be that easy!

Oh, that's the other thing about roller coasters. Once you get off, it doesn't seem so bad.

RELIEF

At school the next day, I slipped Melissa the box (charmingly cardboard and blue, I guess to radiate calm or something), and felt that everything was going to be okay.

PINK

I was very wrong. Content with the outcome of my own little ordeal, I just assumed that the universe would fall into place, when I should have been looking in a completely different direction. Like to the results of the pregnancy test.

Can you fail a pregnancy test? I guess it all depends on whether you want to be pregnant or not. For fourteen-year-olds, it's an automatic F if it turns up pink, no bonus points, no extra credit.

And if pregnancy is bad, then Melissa flunked straight out of school. Even after a retake. Pink, pink, pink.

I was over at her house when she got the results. You're supposed to pee on a little tab and then wait a few minutes before you look at it. I'd read the directions pretty thoroughly on the bus after school, so thoroughly, in fact, that I could probably get a Ph.D. in this stuff. Not that I'd want one.

I went straight to Melissa's house, and we waited together until her mother left for her book club at four. Melissa's mom (Call me Renee!) had just joined a women's book club a couple of weeks ago. I wasn't surprised. Renee was a book-club type of woman, and I was guessing that she did it for the same reason that she did everything else: because she didn't have anything better to do. Her husband worked until nine every evening (I had Melissa's word on this—I'd never seen the man at home, myself), and Renee was left at home all day. She had been a paralegal, but sacrificed her pseudodegree to the more pressing obligations of childbirth and homemaking. Personally, I think she was cheated. What's the point of being a home-mom if you only have one kid? One teenage kid, at that. I asked Melissa about that once, and she said that her mother really *wanted* to have more children, but that her dad had put his foot down. Poor Renee. My mom, on the other hand, certainly does *not* want any more children . . . hell, I'm not even sure she wanted me.

Between three and four, before her mother had left the house, Melissa wouldn't eat anything. She wouldn't even sit down. She just fidgeted around the room with the radio blasting on a hard rock station, which I finally turned down, because I could practically see my brain sloshing around up in my head, and we both stared halfheartedly at old issues of teen magazines.

I watched her as she instinctively assumed the poses of the various models in the magazines. She'd been working on her "look" all summer.

When I heard her mother slam the door, I nearly shoved Melissa into the bathroom in my anxiety. I had a headache.

Six minutes later, I heard sobbing.

Ten minutes later, I heard the lock click on the bathroom door.

Fifteen minutes later, I was whispering consoling things into the keyhole.

Twenty minutes later, Melissa spoke up for the first time. "It's not fair!" she said, and resumed sobbing.

I lost track of time after that. I sat down on Melissa's bed and listened to her cry, absolutely petrified about what that might mean. I couldn't seem to get off the bed once I'd sat down. It was like I was frozen solid. I thought about what I'd do if I were a TV personality: maybe I'd go into the kitchen and get her a glass of water? Knock quietly and coo at her until she came out? Call her parents? Pick the lock?

Melissa hurled herself out of the bathroom just as I was looking about for a lock pick. Her mascara was running in snaky lines down her face, and her cheeks were a dark red.

"It was pink, Jaime! It was pink!"

I had inferred as much.

"There's no need for you to shout, Melissa, it's just—"

"I'm going to have a baby, Jaime. You have to help me!"

"Melissa, you may or may not actually have a baby."

"What do you mean I may not actually have a baby? I'm pregnant, do you understand that? I'm pregnant and I'm Catholic—I'm not having an abortion!"

"I didn't say abortion!" I shouted, raising my voice for the first time. She looked startled. "You don't have to be this dramatic right now! Nothing ever gets *done* when you're being dramatic! There's lots of options. We could do lots of things. We just have to think."

"Dramatic?" she whispered, her eyes narrowing. "You think I'm just being dramatic?" Her voice was sounding slightly dangerous now, escalating to a higher pitch with every word. "You think the test, the p-pregnancy is just my being *dramatic*?"

"I didn't mean that, I just think—"

"All you ever do is think! You don't understand what this means for me. You just don't get it—my parents, my life . . ."

"Melissa . . ."

"You think you know everything. This is just another problem to you!"

"You're right, it is a problem, but we can fix it, we can make it better, we just can't do it by throwing fits."

"Throwing fits?"

"Oh, you know what I–"

"You're right, this is a problem. Except it's never going to get better and you're not going to fix it. It's *my* problem. And you–you don't have anything to do with it!"

"Melissa, if you just calm down–"

"Get out!" she screamed. "Get out of my room!" She backed me into the doorway, and when I turned around, she slammed the door behind me.

TUESDAY

Tuesday is the worst day of the entire week. I don't think it really gets much worse than a Tuesday: it's not Monday so the novelty's gone, and its not quite Wednesday, so you're not at the halfway point yet. This morning was freezing cold, and I waited for Melissa in front of the library, shivering and looking stupid all by myself. I'd dragged myself out of bed and to campus early that morning, because I'd assumed that Melissa would want to talk to me early, as she usually does when something has upset her.

Apparently, she wasn't going to let a pregnancy spoil her sleeping habits.

Either that or she was still not speaking to me.

When I'd gotten home the night after our fight, I'd sat down by the telephone and tried to figure it out. Everything had happened so quickly: first she was telling me she was pregnant and needed my help, and then she was screaming at me to get out of her room. I thought it must have been my fault, as usual. I dialed her number twice but never let it ring. I was so upset that I didn't go downstairs for dinner but resolved to catch the early bus the next morning to try to speak to her.

So I blew hot air onto my aching fingers and counted the number of remaining leaves on the tree near the administration building, waiting for Melissa to show.

Twenty minutes later she rolled up in her dad's car, and she didn't wave. I forgot about the cold and searched her expression like it held the secrets of the stars.

From a distance, she looked like her normal cheerful self. But I could see something funny in her eyes . . . an emptiness, almost, that hadn't been there before. I supposed the tears had stopped out of physical necessity, but the sadness hadn't, so she was crying inside. Like dying people bleed. My stomach, my most faithful anxiety meter, was aching already.

"Melissa . . . ," I started. I didn't finish the sentence, but we both knew what I meant.

"I don't care," she said.

Translation—I care! I care!

"Did you tell your parents?"

"No. I'll never tell my parents anything about this."

Good luck.

"Well, I think you should tell them," I started weakly, but she had already split for history. I stood stock-still in the hallway for a moment, feeling the blood rush to my cheeks. I looked down at my schedule, printed nicely in green ink on my right palm. My first period was English. Yippee.

Of all subjects to have bright and early on a Tuesday, English is definitely the worst. It makes my brain hurt.

During English, while Ms. Robert talked on and on about some play or other in a flatline monotone, I pondered the mysteries of the universe. For me, these consisted of: 1. Why Melissa and I stay friends. 2. What boys do to their hair to make it to stick up like that every morning. 3. My mother. And of course: 4. What I want to be (when I grow up or otherwise).

Today I didn't get past the first mystery, but this was made up for by the fact that I pretty much made the biggest philosophical breakthrough of my life on that one. It took me all of English (which is disguised as a forty-minute period but really lasts until sometime around November), but I basically concluded that Melissa and I are friends because we've always been friends. Ever since I can remember, she's been that little bit of drama in my plain oatmeal life, someone who shines and really stands out to the world. People notice her, all the time, for her looks, for her attitude, for her general superstar glow. People overlook me, and I don't mind, really, but when I'm with her, it's like I absorb some of that glow right into my skin, and people notice me, too. We used to play behind my house, and she would sing while we played, in that perfect, beautiful voice of hers that makes people say "My!" or "What a talent you have there!" and want to get her autograph in advance for when she's famous for something someday.

I really should be jealous. And sometimes I am. In any case, we're still friends. It's some sort of social anomaly—a complete mystery. But I guess I can't worry about it too much, because if Melissa and I are friends because we've always been friends, then I suppose that means we always will be. We'd had fights before. Doesn't everyone? Nasty words wash off with the rain, I knew.

"Please turn to page one thirty-eight," said Ms. Robert.

●

The period after lunch was my next period with Melissa. It was drama class, the most pointless class of the day, therefore Melissa's favorite and my least favorite. The room is slightly claustrophobic, as I've always thought befits a drama teacher. The claustrophobia adds to the intensity of the action, or something like that. The walls are off-white, like the walls of every other classroom in the school, and it has tranquil, mood-blue carpeting that has always reminded me of a flavor of minty gum I used to chew as a kid. Other than a few chairs and a closet full of odds and ends (I hate closets like that—I'm more the color-coding type), the room is bare.

Ms. Roslin was there when we arrived, as usual. Sometimes I think she never leaves that room. But at the same time she has a bit of that city-dweller attitude, like she's been there, done that, and can't stop to chat because she has an appointment elsewhere. She has always struck me as the type of person who would make a great spy.

"Good afternoon," she says, running a hand through perfectly blond hair. She's the only teacher at our high school who even bothers to say good anything anymore. Between earthquakes and gun security issues, I guess it just doesn't seem that important to greet us at the beginning of class.

We stare at Ms. Roslin from our usual social groups, trying to guess why she's smiling so much and what she has in mind for us today. The room is usually configured as such: Snooty Drama Queens on the right (not including Melissa), and Nerdy Shakespeareans on the left (not including me), and the boys—all *three* of them, who we mostly suspect came for the Snooty Drama Queens.

First on the list as far as boys are concerned is Greg Williams. (Keep in mind he's not first for any particular reason, he wasn't even the first to come to my mind. Well, maybe he was, but that doesn't really mean anything.) Greg is sixteen, and he's a sophomore. He's been scoring the romantic leads since he started taking drama in middle school. There has been much speculation as to why, but most say that it's because he's the tallest and best-looking boy in the drama program. Others say it's because his dad owns practically every business in the city. The minority say that it's because he can act.

If Greg Williams is first (mind, he isn't first for a reason), then Michael Bates is definitely second on the list. Michael fancies himself a very talented and important Shakespearean voice in the modern world. Ms. Roslin fancies him a supporting actor. He likes to pause for a minute or two between each line to add emotional weight, and he also likes to burst into tears for no apparent reason at all. He has been known to say "May I take your order, sir?" while spilling tears. I've always thought that he and Melissa should date sometime, but of course I'd never say that out loud.

Zach Miller (short for Zachery) likes to read plays, fiddle with sets, and go to the theater, but otherwise has no business being in drama class. Speaking in public (or even in front of the class) seems to thoroughly overwhelm him. He doesn't have much flair for acting, either. So basically he sits in the back of the room wearing a T-shirt of some obscure eighties band and stares into space.

Most of the time Melissa and I make up our own social group during drama. We nod politely to everyone coming our way (actually I nod politely and Melissa glares politely), but we both have made it clear that we will not separate from each other to go to the groups we really "belong" in.

Today Melissa is sitting next to Alyssa, Snooty Drama Queen-in-Chief.

"Today," says Ms. Roslin, "we will be auditioning for the winter play." Be still, my heart. "Auditions will continue tomorrow after school for all those receiving callbacks. Don't be discouraged if you fail to receive a lead this year . . . we have to keep in mind all matters of seniority and schedule." She smiles widely at us.

Translation—Let's take this one word by word. Seniority: the same people who played leads last year will get leads this year. Schedule: I don't have time to coach any newbies.

"The play will be one with a small cast . . . due to the, um, disappointing size of our high school group this year." She says this while staring pointedly at the boys, as though blaming them for not having more friends.

"How small?" asks a Shakespearean nervously. Shakespeareans never get the really good parts anyway.

"Oh"—she gestures airily—"six parts and crew. This year I will also be choosing a *director* from one of our men. Which is only fair, because there are *no male parts.*" Gasps are heard around the room.

Snooty Drama Queens: What kind of a play is *that?*

Shakespeareans: Good, more for us.

Men: So what time does this period end?

"Any questions?"

"What's the play?" Melissa asks, but not like she cares. Her tone surprises me, and I turn to look at her. She refuses to respond to my questioning look, and I am forced to look away, wondering where my telepathic powers are when I need them.

I really need to know what someone is supposed to do when their pregnant best friend who they care very deeply about is refusing to speak to them.

My mind flicks to Aunt Sheila's phone number on the refrigerator door. Relief washes over me. Sheila can handle it.

"We will be staging *The Effect of Gamma Rays on Man-in-the-Moon Marigolds*," Ms. Roslin says.

Snooty Drama Queens: (Simultaneous gasps) *What?*

Shakespeareans: Must be some New Age thing.

Men: Do we get gamma-ray guns?

DISHWASHING

(MONOLOGUE)

My father left when I was nine years old. It wasn't one of those TV disappearances, where the father runs off with another woman and all the money, leaving his aging wife and daughter to the dogs of poverty. No, he left us everything he owned: his music, his books, Mom's jewelry, his socks. And I know there wasn't another woman, because he loved Mom. So I can only conclude that he had to have left for a real reason . . . like he was secretly dying of a tumor and didn't want us to watch him die. Or he was working for the CIA and got trapped behind enemy lines. Or maybe he gambled away all his money and was too ashamed to tell us so he's trying to get it all back before he comes home. All his relatives lavished gross attention on me for about a year and a half before they realized that I would just as soon be left alone as get presents from any of them. I hardly hear from most of them anymore—it's like they just gave up.

Mom kind of gave up at the same time . . . not on me, really (though sometimes I wish she would), but on life in general. She's a manager of a computer store, but she used to talk about getting a degree in English or something. After dad left, that dream lost all its importance for her.

I feel sorry for her. Not a lot, but enough to keep me doing the dishes every night. That's about the extent of our relationship. The dishes, I mean.

Mom used to have all these chores for me to do. Like doing laundry, making the beds, making dinner, washing the windows, and, on Sundays, the car. She'd always say, "Jaime, we're on our own now. Your dad isn't coming back. I need you to help me, because I can't do it all on my own." Eventually, however, she got sick of running through the list. She'd come home later and later every night from work, and she stopped caring about clean windows, or laundry, or made beds. Soon, she even stopped caring whether or not I brushed my teeth. But the dishes she stuck to. With a vengeance.

I do have one relative who has never given up on me. Actually, I don't think my aunt has ever given up on anything.

My aunt Sheila is the coolest person I know. She's an executive in an office in Silicon Valley and likes to take me out to a steakhouse every time she gets promoted (which is often and generally includes relocation to a higher floor). She has perfect professional-looking business cards with her name on them in silver italics. She paints her nails fire-engine red every day after work and takes me to midnight movies. She reads books for hours in Barnes and Noble, purchasing dozens of hot chocolates per book so they can't kick her out. For Thanksgiving, she makes steamed lobster and tapes a sign to her window that says SAVE THE DAMN TURKEYS.

●

I keep Sheila's phone number on the refrigerator door. It's written in red ink on a Post-it note of emergency listings. And if you need further proof of how much I trust Sheila, you should know that I wrote her number just under 911. Usually she calls me, because her schedule is a mess, but I decided that Melissa's predicament constituted an emergency and dialed her cell phone after school on Tuesday.

"Sheila?"

"Mmm-hmmm."

"This is Jaime." I was confident that she would

know that if I was calling *her* (something I am always hesitant to do) my situation was dire.

There was a pause.

"Oh, Jaime! Do you—want to come over for a while?" Another thing about my aunt—she can sense anxiety in my voice better than I can sense it in my own head.

"Um, yeah, that would be great."

"I'll come pick you up, then," she said without hesitation.

"Thanks."

"Ciao."

Click.

•

We went to Zuka Juice for a health drink and some time to talk. I ordered a Strawberry Snowblast and explained to Aunt Sheila about Melissa's pregnancy while she got a Mango Madness and looked nonplussed. I was surprised that the news hadn't shocked her (as the subject seems to do for most adults), but then, nothing shakes Aunt Sheila. After a couple of moments Zuka juicing in silence, I asked her, "What should I do?"

"Well, first of all, dear, the question is not what should you do, but what should *she* do."

"Yeah, but you know what Melissa's like."

"What Melissa's like has nothing to do with this. You don't need to waste your energy trying to get her to talk to you when she's being too pigheaded to see what's good for her."

"But I can't just do nothing," I said.

"Jaime, as unfortunate as this situation is, it's not worth your losing sleep over it. My advice is that you don't get involved. Especially if she continues acting the way she has been."

"I don't know," I said. "I mean, she's my best friend."

"It's not always easy to look out for your own interests. But it doesn't mean that it's not necessary. Do you have any idea who got her pregnant in the first place?"

The question caught me off guard and put me in a bit of a mood, despite the comforting juice shake in my hand. I was still bitter that Melissa wouldn't cough up a name. But I figured that he (whoever he was) should be doing *something* to help her out. Shouldn't he? I mean, she didn't get pregnant all by herself. Of course, since she wouldn't tell me who it was, it wasn't like I could do anything about it. And, according to Sheila, I really shouldn't be trying to do anything about it anyway.

I shook my head and chewed thoughtfully on my straw. It's a habit I inherited from Sheila.

"It doesn't matter anyway," Sheila said. "If she's pregnant, she's pregnant."

"You know she'll never be able to handle this on her own."

"So tell her parents," said Sheila. I almost choked on my Strawberry Snowblast at the very suggestion.

"I would never do that!" I said. And it was true.

Sheila shrugged and said, "Well, whatever you do, just remember that it's her problem."

I flinched at the phrase. *Her problem.* Why couldn't I just take Sheila's advice and let it go at that?

I spluttered about in several pools of argument for a while, but it didn't make any difference. Sheila tapped her bright red fingernails and countered every move I made. As she sat there with perfect makeup, prim and authoritative as ever, it even seemed like I could follow her suggestions. But after she dropped me off at home and the phone started ringing and my mother started shouting, I knew I was still drowning.

DREAMS

My health class teacher handed me back my Dream Sheet today and told me to redo it. She said it was unsatisfactory. I asked her if I could take it home with me, and she said that would be fine.

"Really try to put some effort into this, Jaime," she said.

When I got home I put off looking at the sheet until it was dark outside. Then I spent an hour or two staring out my windows, tapping my pencil against my teeth. The noise made Jake nervous, and he writhed around in his cage until I noticed him and stopped.

What is your most powerful dream?

I've had dreams before. I wanted to open a family pizza place with my father and pretend I was Italian, but that went down the drain the day he left. I wanted my mother to buy me my own art studio when I was ten years old, but we didn't have enough money. I wanted to design my own fashion line at thirteen and be the youngest fashion guru in the business, but you know where that one went. I also wanted to be a ballerina when I was twelve years old but copped out because I was too lazy.

So I'm not a ballerina, I don't have my own art studio, there isn't a family business (hell, there's hardly any family), and I don't have my own fashion line. Where does that leave me? you wonder. What am I, then?

Average.

I got up to brush my teeth, leaving the sheet blank on my desk. What does it matter what my dreams are? Melissa has a dream. She wants to be a model. What is she?

She's pregnant.

At fourteen.

A statistic.

CALL

The phone rang so late tonight that my mother refused
to pick it up. I picked it up instead, after making record
time down the stairs and almost colliding with our new
sliding glass door, because I was hoping it was Melissa.
She hadn't spoken to me all day, and I'd taken Sheila's
advice and not gone out of my way to try to speak to
her. I think that startled Melissa a little. Maybe she was
finally calling to see what was up.

I took a deep breath before putting the receiver to
my ear, panting. If it was Melissa, I had to tell her that I
still wanted to be her friend but that I couldn't really
help her on this one. She needed to find "adult aid,"

somewhere, somehow. Sheila was right—my involvement wouldn't help anything. Would it? Standing there, instants away from actual communication, I wasn't so sure.

When I heard the voice on the other end of the telephone line, I almost dropped the receiver. It wasn't Melissa. It was Greg Williams. I sure wasn't in Kansas anymore.

"Oh, hi," I said. I was still panting from my trip downstairs, so I held my breath. I learned a very important life lesson there—if you hold your breath when you're panting, you start gasping. I held the phone as far from my mouth as possible. "Um, so what's up?" I gasped. Wow, that was clever.

"Jaime, I'm calling about the audition. I think you did really great."

"Really?" Suddenly I couldn't find my vocabulary.

"Yeah, really. Anyway, we're supposed to pair up for callbacks tomorrow. You know, for leads. Girl and guy."

"Callbacks? I don't even think I made it."

"Oh, come on, Jaime. You were great. You were like in a zone or something. Didn't you see Ms. Roslin's face? You're a sure bet." Ladies and gentlemen, place your bets, please.

"Well, okay—I mean, you did really well—I mean great, too." Shoot me now. Just take the damn phone away.

"Thanks."

Complete silence. I could have killed for some static.

"So about the pairs—"

"Yes! Yeah, I'd love to."

"Cool, we'll be great together. Just remember to sign us up in the morning, okay?"

Would I ever. "Okay."

"Bye."

It took me about a minute and a half to acknowledge that conversation as a reality. Greg Williams wanted to pair off with me for callback scenes tomorrow! Wow. I mean, truly wow. It was completely surreal. One of those things that happens for no rhyme or reason, but does—almost like the stars sent it to you, just because you're there and you're lucky. Like a director who showed up at your house after weeks of auditioning to give you that big break that would move you from starlet to starlight in minutes, give you dark sunglasses, silk scarves, an affected accent, and a Corvette named Charlie, after Charlie Chaplin. I think in the dictionary they call it a miracle.

Suddenly I felt like there should be music.

"Jaime? Who was it?"

"Just a—friend. From school. Calling—"

"At this hour?"

"Never mind."

Against my will, I was too warm and fuzzy inside to explain.

CRUSH

Despite how it looks, I don't actually have a crush on Greg. Or at least, not a crush in the usual sense of the word . . . but try to wrap your mind around this:

Have you ever felt that something is so impossible that it's barely even real to you at all? Or felt that something is so far away that you can dismiss the possibility of its ever reaching you, and in doing so, dismiss the possibility of its existence before you even consider it possible? I suppose if I had a crush on Greg, that would be the type of crush I would have. As in, "Yeah, right."

"Forget it."

"In your dreams."

You know, I can't ever really remember having a dream—a dream dream, like at night—for sure. I can vaguely remember the strange, illogical thoughts I had right before I fell asleep, or right after I woke up, but nothing in between. Everyone else seems to dream—they dream wonderful things, or horrible things, and share them with their friends. But for me, it's like I don't even *exist* at night. Like there's nothing there.

I don't have a crush on Greg Williams. Really. I swear.

Cross my heart and hope to . . . Wow, when you write it down, that expression seems so much more serious.

SOLITAIRE

It's Sunday, and I haven't heard from Melissa all weekend. I almost didn't know what to do with myself. I ended up spending a lot of time playing solitaire on my mom's computer, trying not to worry about it. Like that's ever worked.

ATOM

The way my morning goes almost always dictates the quality of my day. It sets the mood, sets the tone, you know? And if the tone is nasty or the mood is dark, it's just too bad for me. On Monday morning, I felt like I was raining inside.

"Mom, we're out of Cheerios," I said.

"So eat Froot Loops," she replied distractedly, dressing for work.

"We're out of those, too."

"So eat fruit, Jaime, be creative."

I ate fruit and waited for Mom to come down to the table. When she finally did, her hair was still wet and she was still trying to button up. I should have spotted the walking disaster the minute it came down the stairs. Instead, I said, "Guess what? I think I'm getting a call-back today. It'll be the first time ever."

"Mmm-hmm."

"So I'm going to sign up this morning. For me and Greg."

"That's nice, Jaime." Mom was already up from the breakfast table and searching for her keys. "Clear your plate."

I got up from the table, slammed the plate into the sink as loud as I could, and ran up the stairs. Why do I even bother? I kept thinking. She doesn't care any-more. Once maybe she did. But now we're barely re-lated.

"Young lady! What do you think you're doing? Get back here this instant!" I heard my mother shout up to me.

It went downhill from there. And I couldn't stop thinking that a little interest on my mom's part could have gone a long way.

I got to school early to sign Greg and me up on Ms. Roslin's front door. Like Greg had anticipated, both our names were on the list. Normally I would have been ec-static. More than ecstatic—exultant. But as it was, I still felt cold and unhappy inside. So I put a check by our names and filled in a time slot. And that was all. Melissa was there early too, but I avoided her searching eyes and pretended I didn't see her. She looked as forlorn as ever—but it was only her third day being for certain pregnant, so what could you expect? I told myself she'd get used to it. It wasn't my problem. I had other things to worry about.

First period I had science. I tried to take notes (no, really, I did), but my heart wasn't in it. I couldn't even spell *element* right the first time. Second period I had math. I can't even remember what we were supposed to be learning.

Third period was P.E., my only class that day with Melissa. My locker was across from hers, and I found myself hoping I'd see her before I changed.

Across the room, a group of girls were having an intensely giggly conversation.

"Well, she's definitely gone *somewhere,* hasn't she," I heard Alyssa say coyly, glancing at me surreptitiously. That's what set me on my guard.

I heard giggles from the other side of the lockers. I looked up at them, braced for trouble. Except they didn't seem to be talking about me.

"She was *crying,*" Rachel pitched in. "I mean, really *bawling.*"

More giggling.

"Well, I guess we know what that's all about," I heard someone say.

"*Who* that's all about!" Alyssa answered. Everyone seemed to think this was very clever.

"Where is she now?" someone asked.

"In the bathroom, crying her eyes out," said Alyssa.

I looked around for Melissa. She still hadn't come into the room.

My mind raced, and I couldn't quite catch up with the bunny. What was going on? I knew there was only one way I could find out. I had to get back down to the bathrooms.

●

I am not good with people in tears. In fact, I tend to just make it worse. I try to be soothing, of course, but years of being on the other end of sympathy has always made my cooing sound terribly insincere.

I've decided that I am a clay doormat—I melt with the rain.

And when I got to the bathroom, Melissa was raining, all right. Half the things she said I couldn't even understand, but I got the gist. I also understood that Alyssa and her friends' hypotheses about the problem had been way off the mark.

Melissa had thrown up into the toilet during first period. She said it took her a while to understand what was happening, but she knew it had to do with the baby.

"Ugly, stupid, stupid baby! It had to be morning sickness, Jaime. Stupid baby!"

"Don't say that," I mumbled, patting her back.

"You can't tell me what to say! You're not pregnant! You don't understand!"

She was right. I didn't understand.

"What kind of friend are you?" she demanded. "You've been avoiding me for the last three days."

"No, I . . ." But of course it was true.

"Is it because I'm pregnant? Does that make me not good enough for you?"

"Of course that's not—"

"Well, you're wrong. Because I'm not like you. I'm—I'm not ugly, and spiteful, and ashamed of my friends. . . ."

I felt like I'd been slapped. I moved away from Melissa, to the other side of the bathroom. The room felt claustrophobic.

"I'm—really sorry, Melissa," I said, on the verge of tears myself. Doormats do not cry easily. People step on us and wipe their dirt on us all the time, and we don't ever cry. But this doormat suddenly felt like she was losing something important, and she could not understand why.

Melissa was right. I would never understand what she was going through.

I opened the door to leave.

"Wait, Jaime, wait—"

"What?"

"I didn't really mean that. I'm just . . . angry, that's all."

I looked back at her, her face red and strained, her eyes lost under her sagging lids and brimming tears, her hair disheveled for the first time since elementary school.

"Don't worry about it. I'm sorry," I said. I'm always sorry. But I took a deep breath and said, "You're right about everything, you know. I was avoiding you because–because I felt like it just wasn't my problem. And it's not–I mean, it's yours. But you're my best friend and I've decided I want to help. I really do."

Melissa blinked at me.

I walked away.

●

The wrong thing to do is only seldom the right thing to do. I wasn't sure, but I felt like maybe I'd found one of those situations where it's better to go for the wrong thing for all the right reasons. Yet I knew it was only the right thing to do because I had chosen to do it–I'd made the decision all on my own. Sheila would understand that. She had to.

By the time I got to art, my last-period class, under the cumulative weight of my fight with my mom that morning and the episode in the bathroom that afternoon, I felt like something was slowly squeezing all the air out of my lungs.

My classmates, I discovered, are much more empathetic than I ever gave them credit for. Though they acted like dogs on a gossip hunt, I was at least thankful that I looked as bad as I felt.

I felt like I was seconds away from death by suffocation.

Several people were brave enough to ask me what was wrong. I either said I had a cold (sure, fine, whatever) or that I would rather not talk about it. The majority of the class just stayed out of my way, snickering occasionally and wondering when I was going to blow. Some, however, seemed genuinely concerned. For example, Zach Miller.

We have homeroom together, and most of our classes. He's an artist, or wants to be, and is the quiet yet shining star of every art room. Being a bit of an aspiring artist myself, I usually consider him competition. Now, in last-period art, he sat next to me, and I looked up.

"What's up, Jaime?" he asked quietly. He always speaks quietly.

"I don't want to . . ." I looked over at him, and really looked at him. I saw a glimmer of concern. Real emotion? It must be the heat. Nonetheless, I took a deep breath and told him, "I'm having some trouble with a friend."

He nodded like he knew what I was talking about.

"I'm sorry."

"Me too."

End of conversation.

I was still trying not to cry when the time came for my callback audition. And trying to keep yourself from having an all-out salty breakdown is harder to do than it seems. In order to not cry, when you really feel you have to, you have to walk around with this burning ball of radiant energy caught in your chest and blink rapidly to keep the water from spilling. Worse, a cry is unpredictable and can be triggered at any moment. For example, the sight of a dead cricket might be the end for me.

"Ready for the scene?" Greg asked me, pulling away from a cluster of very miffed Snooty Drama Queens. Alyssa pouted.

"Yeah, I guess so."

"Great. We'll be great. You did sign us up, right?"

"Um, yeah. . . ."

I glanced at Melissa. She didn't have a partner. I saw Zach glancing around too. I struggled for a while to make eye contact with him, and when I finally managed it, I jerked my head toward Melissa. He nodded. She needed a partner. He settled himself down next to Melissa and shook her hand. She looked no less than thrilled.

Of the four or five of us in the room for the callbacks, I felt ridiculously lucky to be with Greg.

"Partners! I'm giving you a number. When I call that number, you both will come front and center, and the female partner will read any scene I choose. Men will direct. You've all seen me do it, so it shouldn't be too much trouble. Of course I don't expect you to be perfect, just add your ideas to what the actress should do to run her lines smoother, and we'll see. Questions?"

Greg was beaming, but I hated the very idea. How were you supposed to "direct" one actress? It would be more like coaching.

The guys in the class were looking very confused.

We began.

●

Ms. Roslin: Number one! Greg, Jaime, Act one, page thirty-one, where Beatrice starts. Got it? Front and center.

Me/Beatrice: "Science, science, science! Don't they teach our misfits anything anymore? Anything decent and meaningful and sensitive?"

Greg: I think this is a very touchy moment, Beatrice. Put some gut into it!

I figure *gut* means talk louder. Either that or find a Five & Diner.

Me/Beatrice: "DO YOU KNOW WHAT I'D BE NOW IF IT WASN'T FOR THIS MUD POOL I GOT SUCKED INTO?"

Greg: No, Beatrice, it's *building*! Start slow! And move around more, like you mean it!

Ms. Roslin: Good advice, Greg! Zach and Melissa, switch! Where Jaime left off!

Greg glares at me as we sit down. *Stupid,* his eyes say, *can't you act?* I feel like crying once again.

Melissa/Beatrice: "One minute I'm the best dancer in school . . ."

Melissa is really into it. Ms. Roslin clasps her hands,

and Zach mumbles something that sounds like "Good. Um, projection, yeah, project your voice and–" But she's already moved on. She spoke for a long time, it seemed to me. Then came the next group. And the next. Greg still glaring. And the next. Melissa is called up again. And then so are we. Greg *smiles.* Smiles like that can give perfectly healthy teenage girls a heart murmur.

Ms. Roslin: Okay, Jaime, try this. Act one, page one, second paragraph for Tillie. Greg, give her a cue.

My insides are writhing and screaming, *Don't blow this. Don't blow this!*

Greg cues.

Me/Tillie: "And this small part–"

Greg: Come on, Tillie! What's up with that weak crap!

Me/Tillie: "–of me–"

Greg: Put some *emotion* into it!

Me/Tillie: "–was then a whisper of the earth."

Greg: Louder again. Support your breathing!

Ms. Roslin: Very good, Greg.

Greg: And enunciate.

Ms. Roslin: I think the problem lies in projection.

Greg: But if you really listen, her words are a bit slurred. . . .

My radiant ball of salt-energy is seconds away from exploding. I have to do something, and fast, or risk embarrassment in front of the entire class.

Me: Can you both just shut up a minute!

Both he and Ms. Roslin go silent.

Instinctively I look to Melissa, who knits her eyebrows, wondering what I'm up to. My eyes slide to Zach, sitting next to her. He's looked up at the stage for the first time since his botched audition.

Numb before my own audacity, I keep reading in an effort to finish what I'd started.

Me/Tillie: ". . . When there was life, perhaps this part of me got lost in a fern that was crushed and covered until it was coal. And then it was a diamond millions of years later—it must have been a diamond as beautiful as the star from which it had first come.

"Or perhaps this part of me became lost in a terrible beast, or became part of a huge bird that flew above the primeval swamps.

"And he said this thing was so small—this part of me was so small it couldn't be seen—but it was there from the beginning of the world.

"And he called this bit of me an atom. And when he wrote the word, I fell in love with it.

"Atom.

"*Atom*.

"What a beautiful word."

I finished. I set the script down. Ms. Roslin and Greg were still sitting in stunned silence. My cheeks turned to flame as I regretted my poorly timed outburst. It was funny, though—while I was reading and babbling on, I'd felt something strange, and the strange something had had to do with the words printed on that page. I had felt stronger, more powerful, more alive. Of course, now the feeling was gone and the entire class was staring at me like I'd escaped from the zoo. Could I just say I'd had a long day?

Ms. Roslin looked at me hard. I felt like she was sending a sword through my belly, and Greg, with his matching glare of *Oh my god I can't believe you screwed us up,* walked right up to that sword and turned it in my belly.

But then Ms. Roslin began to applaud. Or golf clap, anyway.

"Very–very good, Jaime! Sometimes you have to tell your director when you need to let the artist in you speak! However–next time, maybe not quite so harshly. Greg, very good feedback, very good, but maybe not appropriate in that magnitude for an audition. The actress has to have her chance too, you know."

Translation–Don't worry, Greg, you still got the part.

She laughed, nervously.

"Well, I guess that's good for today, then!"

I left so fast I can't even remember opening the door.

GLOW

The audition results were finally posted today on a kiosk by the gym. I saw Melissa's name on the list, and Greg's. My name was written across from my part– *Tillie!*

The news made my whole day glow. After school got out, I went to see Ms. Roslin, and she handed me a full script, which I read hungrily on the bus home from school.

So here's the deal. Basically, the play is about a girl– Tillie–who wants to be a scientist. She wants to go to school (if you can imagine that), but her mother won't let her (now try and imagine *that*). Tillie's got a special hunger inside her, a hunger for knowledge, and especially for science. Her family members can't understand where that hunger came from, because they certainly don't have it. And so they fight against Tillie's hunger–Tillie's *passion,* I guess you'd say, because they're uneducated, poor, and unhappy.

Tillie's mother, Beatrice, is insane. Or at least going insane. Beatrice has gotten trapped in her memories, the memories of a better time, and she can't bring herself to accept a world she doesn't want to live in. Tillie's sister, Ruth, is crazy too. But she's *really* crazy–as in mentally unbalanced. Sick.

People talk about Tillie's mother like she's sick too. And in a way she is–she just can't leave the past behind, resign herself to a life she hates.

But Tillie, that's me, is the best part of the story, because she's the part that's still hopeful about the world. Because she has the hope that her mother and sister lack, she becomes involved in a school science fair, for which she is growing marigolds–man-in-the-moon-marigolds–and irradiating them with gamma rays.

Mom has seen the play before. Her high school put it on. She teased me about finally getting to be the star after all these years taking drama, but I didn't mind.

It's a great play, she said.

Uh-huh.

No, really, it's a good one.

Thanks, Mom.

Like I'd trust anything performed in the sixties.

DEFINITION

"Pregnancy: 1. The state of carrying developing offspring within the body. 2. The period during which one is pregnant with a same-species fetus. 3. Creativity; inventiveness.

"Fetus: 1. The unborn young of a viviparous vertebrate having basic structural resemblance to the adult animal. 2. In humans, the unborn young from the end of the eighth week after conception to the moment of birth, as distinguished from the earlier embryo."

I don't own any encyclopedias, so researching the topic of pregnancy this weekend was a little harder than I imagined. Let's face it: the dictionary just isn't that informative. However, I did learn one very important thing—or rather, learned what I needed to learn to know one very important thing: I had to find out how long Melissa had been carrying this baby.

Eight weeks and it may be too late for an abortion.

Six months and everyone knows.

Nine months and you have a baby.

BOY

At school the next day, I found my first chance to speak with Melissa during our study hall. I sat down next to her, as far away from the rest of the class as possible. When I saw the librarian picking up a bathroom pass, I started talking.

"Okay, Melissa. So how long have you had this . . . baby?"

"Shhh!" She looked around in a panic. I rolled my eyes. "What, no hello?" she whispered. I knew I'd heard that one in a movie.

"Melissa . . ."

"All right, all right. I can't know for sure, but . . . four weeks minimum."

"Minimum?"

"Minimum."

"Can you give me like a maximum or something? Because four weeks minimum doesn't really narrow it down much for me."

She ignored my sarcasm. When Melissa is in "project" mode, nothing can faze her. "Maximum . . . five weeks. It can't be any more."

I sighed. "So who was it, Melissa? I think I need to know."

"No, you don't."

"Do."

"Don't!"

"Look, how are you supposed to know what I need to—oh, never mind." I took a deep breath. "And you've started feeling sick, like, to your stomach sometimes?"

Melissa opened her mouth to answer but didn't answer quickly enough.

"That'd be morning sickness."

Wait. I didn't say that. I almost jumped out of my skin. Zach was standing right behind me.

"Um, careful," he said, surprised. Melissa looked aghast.

I don't really know what *aghast* means, but I've heard it used a lot in books—mostly cheesy mysteries.

But if anyone looked aghast, then Melissa was ghasting right out of a magazine. As usual.

"You—you were *eavesdropping*!" I said. Suddenly the rest of the study hall was staring at me too. I had a split second to think, Conspiracy! They're all eavesdropping! when I realized I had shouted. The librarian was glaring at me. Really, really glaring. She must have come back from the bathroom, I thought lamely. She pointed at Zach, and at me, and at the door. Zach looked embarrassed about having to leave. I was embarrassed that I had to stay long enough to open the door.

When we got outside, I pointed at him and shouted into his face, "You were *eavesdropping*!" I was having trouble thinking of another line.

"I was not!" he said. "Don't shout—"

"You were, and you have no right to be getting into people's private business like that. That's why we were whispering. Whispering makes it private!"

"You were *not* whispering."

"We were!"

"Well, maybe, but you were doing it loudly!"

"You were standing right behind me, of course it sounded loud!"

"I couldn't help hearing," he mumbled. "I really couldn't. I didn't even think you guys were being *serious.*"

"Yeah, sure." The whole school was so—well, nosy— that I just couldn't stand it any longer. I felt tired. "So now I guess you know. Congratulations, you know."

He looked down. Weird, I'd expected more yelling. But I suspected I sounded too exhausted to be provocative. We sat down on the concrete outside the library, about twelve feet apart. Then I remembered:

"Hey, you knew about the morning sickness."

"Yeah."

"How?"

"My mom was pregnant all last year."

"Oh."

I was quiet for a while.

"Did she have a boy or girl?" I asked.

"Boy. Almost."

"How do you get almost a boy?"

"He died."

"Oh. Sorry."

He tried to accept my apology with a pat on the back, or a hug, or something, but I brushed his hand away. "Do I *look* like a welcome mat?" I snapped.

Zach looked totally confused. Somehow, I didn't blame him.

PREGNANCY

So Zach is in. Part of the brand-new pregnancy club. It would be funny if it wasn't so sad. Here's how it happened:

I called him after dinner–mostly to confirm his secrecy–but he did more than that. He offered to help. At first, I couldn't see that we needed any help. But after about five minutes really thinking about all that a pregnancy entails, I realized we needed all the help we could get.

"In the end, the choices are all Melissa's," he said. "But whatever she wants, we could help her get."

No one in his or her right mind would want to get involved in this. So that means Zach Miller is either very, very crazy, or very, very bored. You would think if he needed a hobby he'd take up basket weaving. Kids these days.

JUICE

I've always been the type of person who worries excessively. I worry about important things, of course, but I also worry about the little things that most people never waste a moment's thought on. Sometimes I agonize over what it means to be alive, what it's all leading up to. Sometimes I agonize over my future, or what I'll be like in my old age, and sometimes I agonize over sunscreen SPFs. But I've almost (almost, mind you) stopped agonizing altogether. All thanks to my aunt Sheila.

I've put trust into Aunt Sheila for a long time now. Whenever I have worries, I tie them up, put them in a brown paper bag, and leave them at her doorstep. She pokes around in them for a while, says, "What are you talking about? There's nothing in there!" and then gives them back to me, along with some advice and a Zuka juice.

Sheila's advice has never yet led me astray. Sometimes I have to interpret it a little, fit it to my own situation, but it's always come out right in the end. So when I was feeling a little shaky over the weekend, I called her up and told her all about what happened between me, Melissa, and Zach.

The story spanned several Zuka juices, because I told it scene by scene, play by play, with all the gory details.

"It's obvious," she said, musing over a Coconut Kaboom. "He likes you."

I blinked in surprise, just barely keeping my brain connected to my tongue long enough to refrain from asking, "Who?"

"When I said 'help me,' I meant about the whole pregnancy thing, not about my love life."

Just like Sheila to miss the entire point of my monologue on purpose.

"Same thing."

"No, it's not."

"Yes, it is."

I shut up and focused on my Citrus Squeeze.

Okay. I can deal with that. As I said, Sheila's always right.

REHEARSAL

"Not bad, Tillie, not bad. But try to make it across the stage a little quicker, and don't stand in front of Janice, because her line's next, and . . ."

Yes, that is Greg. Shouting as usual. But instead of coming back with anything that I would have cause to be embarrassed about later, I just say, "Okay."

"Great!" he says, and claps his hands. He's been slowly suffering a mutation of his own—from Greg Williams to director Greg H. Williams. He's been speaking loudly lately, clapping his hands a lot, and walking with an extra swagger. Or was that there before? He's even dressing the part, in wifebeaters and shoes that click, and I think it makes him look like a lumberjack. But Alyssa loves it. Or, as she says, loooves it. And she gets plenty of time to check it out, too . . . she scored the part of Ruth, the final member of our cast.

Ever since Ms. Roslin relinquished (or mostly relinquished) control of rehearsals to Greg so that he could become the first ever student director in our high school's history, things have been very strange in the drama department. Greg takes up a lot of rehearsal time talking about "efficiency issues" and other things that I generally chalk up to nonsense. As a result, we have longer rehearsals than we've ever had before. I used to catch the late bus while I was rehearsing for the winter play, but now my mom has to drive to school to pick me up. Let's just say that puts neither of us in a good mood.

The members of the drama class who didn't get parts all got black T-shirts that say CREW MEMBER instead. Basically *crew member* means they get to sit around and eat while pretending to be doing "advance planning" for the sets, lighting, and sound.

Zach came in today while Alyssa, as Ruth, was rehearsing her first monologue. I wondered if it was hard to stay in character and shoot flirty looks at the director at the same time.

Zach sat down next to me on the backstage floor. He had a baguette sandwich and chips. He gave the chips to me.

"What's up?" he asked. I knew by that he meant, How's Melissa?

"Not too much," I answered. By which I meant, She hasn't said anything to me.

"Maybe we should talk to her."

"Yeah, maybe so," I said wearily. The long rehearsal hours had really started to get to me over the past week, and I hadn't made much of an effort to do anything more complicated than my homework. I thought maybe I'd try calling Melissa later in the evening.

I hear Ms. Roslin shout a suggestion to Greg. He clears his throat, and that's the signal for the cast to get up and get ready for a new scene. "Let's get Beatrice out here for the last telephone call," he says.

No one says anything.

Zach and I glance at each other.

Beatrice does not appear.

"Beatrice?" Greg says. "Is Beatrice here?" Slightly irritated now, he shouts, "Beatrice! Get out here!"

Beatrice, aka Melissa, still has not made her fashionably late entrance. I look around. She's not here. She has not shown up for rehearsal.

Zach looks around wildly, and I check my watch. It's already five o'clock. Where is Melissa?

We booked out of there as soon as Greg gave up on Beatrice's ever showing up. He called off rehearsal for that day but swore revenge for next time.

Melissa was getting sick in the girls' bathroom. Really, really sick. She kept saying, "I want to go home!" and "Stupid, stupid baby!" I patted her head over the bowl for a half hour before I remembered Zach. I opened the bathroom door and peeked around the corner.

"There you are!" I said. "What are you doing out here?"

"Well I can't go in *there*," he said, and nodded anxiously toward the girls' room door. I'd learned to interpret his nods as a sign of his deep distress.

"Why not—oh! Don't be silly. There's no one in there anyway."

"Well, not now, there isn't."

Exasperated, I said, "It's a school bathroom. And school is over. Why would anyone else be in there?"

He just stood in front of me, tapping his foot. He must have been tapping it hard, too, because New Balances don't make a whole hell of a lot of noise. Taking some deep yoga breaths and counting to ten, I finally grabbed his arm and tried to tug him inside.

"Hey!" he shouted, surprised, but was able to pull away.

He narrowed his eyes at me.

"Okay, look," I said, at the end of my fuse. "You have to come in and see what's wrong with Melissa. You promised you'd help us. So at least come take a look at her and then you can leave." He shook his head, so I flung the door open and pointed to the stall where Melissa was.

"*That* is Melissa. She is having a baby. Neither of us

71

knows what to do with it, or when. She is *at least* in her fifth week–"

"*At most,* Jaime!" A muffled voice cried from the stall, indignant.

"Okay, at most, and she is going to start showing in two months." Who says I don't learn anything in drama?

Melissa slouched out of the bathroom stall and sat down on the tile floor, putting her head between her knees. Zach, staring at me like I was a circus elephant, inched inside the bathroom and sat down next to her. I guess he didn't know that doormats carry bugles for emergencies.

He turned his eyes to Melissa.

"Um . . . okay. There's really nothing you can do about the way you feel right now," he said, "except for maybe taking some generic stomach flu pills. Don't let this stuff scare you too much–it's morning sickness, I mean, it's normal."

"Since when was this morning?" Melissa spat.

"It's not always a morning thing, it's just a stupid name."

"Melissa," I said. "When did you start feeling sick today?"

"A few minutes ago," she said.

"But why didn't you come to rehearsal?"

Melissa didn't say anything for a moment. And then she looked up at me with sad eyes. "Jaime," she said. "We've already had a week of rehearsal. And I just can't be in that room anymore! You don't understand what it's like, and I can't tell you why, it's just—I hate rehearsal. Every minute of it. I couldn't take it today, so I went to the library. Then I started feeling sick, so I came here."

I looked down at my shoes. Something was trying to work its way through my mind.

"Well," said Zach, and I looked up again. "Considering that rehearsal has been called off on your account, I think we should use this time to talk about—er, our long-term issues."

"Okay," said Melissa, watching him expectantly.

"Er," he said, glancing nervously around the room.

"Okay, okay," I said. "Let's go to the library!"

While I had been too tired after rehearsals to do anything but crash every night, Zach had done some research, and he had a plan. In the library that day, he outlined Melissa's options like a story in a Choose Your Own Adventure book:

"Well, the first thing we should do is call Planned Parenthood and set you up with an appointment. They will probably be able to recommend some abortion clinics if you want to do it that way." At the suggestion of abortion, Melissa shook her head vehemently.

"Or they can give you some advice on how to break the news to your parents, how to deal with the stress, and where to find special clinics for teenage pregnancies."

Again Melissa shook her head, apparently at the suggestion that she tell her parents anything.

"Of course, you can also get your parents involved straight away, and get checked out by your doctor. To get access to a real doctor, you're definitely going to have to tell your parents."

Or shoot them, I thought.

Again Melissa shook her head, and let out a heavy, dramatic sigh.

"If I were to get an abortion," she said, "could I get one without my parents knowing anything?"

Zach was quiet for a minute. "Well, yes, I suppose," he finally said. "But you'd need money, for starters, and then a doctor who would do it without a parent's signature. But, look, there's no guarantee that a secret abortion would be sanitary or painless or anything. They're just not safe!"

We were all quiet a minute, reviewing Melissa's options.

"Let's just take this one step at a time, then," I said. "I guess that puts Planned Parenthood first on the list."

"Where is Planned Parenthood?" Melissa asked.

"Um . . ."

"I think there's one in Silicon Valley," said Zach.

"Maybe it's not first on the list, then," said Melissa.

"Okay," Zach said, checking his watch. "I've got to go. I'll see you guys tomorrow."

No one said anything. He paused for a moment and then left the room.

I sat down where he had been. "It's going to be okay," I told her. I would have hugged her, but doormats are not touchy-feely type people. She opened her mouth to speak, and I expected her to say something about the baby, or about how screwed she was for life, but instead she said, "You know, he's cute."

I stared at her openmouthed. I've had a lot of crushes over the time that we've been best friends, and I've faithfully told her about every one. She always acts disparaging, pointing out their faults—bushy eyebrows, a broken nose, too many zits. I felt like this was my big chance to tell her about someone she'd approve of, but I wasn't sure how to go about it. Instead of tucking my secret under my doormat and hiding, however, I pursued it in that roundabout, struggling, ineloquent way that people have when their brain disconnects from the rest of them:

"Yeah, I know he's cute," I said. "And I actually—well, Sheila told me something yesterday. She said 'He probably likes you, too.' " There. I'd said it. And I was blushing.

Melissa's eyes went wide, as I knew they would. But instead of discouraging me, and instead of acting surprised, she said, "Oh my god, that's great, he *does*?"

"Yeah. Yeah, you know, he does," I said, enthusiastically. Probably a little too enthusiastically. "I guess he maybe really does."

"Well, that's great!" she said. "And all this time I had no idea that he was hiding some *crush* on me. But now it all makes sense!"

Time stopped for a second, and the spotlight was on

the doormat. I knew I was supposed to do something dramatic, like fleeing the bathroom and slamming the door, but all I could do was try and remember what she had just said. She'd said *me*. Me. Me, Melissa.

I realized I should be angry. I should be surprised. Even upset. I should blow my top in jealousy, and rage, and explain to her what my real suspicions were, that I thought he liked *me*. I should have been offended that she would think Sheila and I discussed her that way. I should have been offended that she saw more love in herself than in me.

But I wasn't. I really, truly, wasn't. I just felt kind of tired—like I'd been stepped on too many times and it was no longer worth it to complain.

The spotlight quivered, faded, and died. Bye, bye, Broadway.

PLANNED

Saturday I painted my nails fire-engine red. The whole time, Jake, my iguana, stared angrily at me with his beady little eyes, protesting the fumes. I apologized but didn't stop painting. I felt like I needed all the undoormattishness I could get, and though I have seen doormats in very interesting colors, I have never in my life seen one in fire-engine red. It would be like an oxymoron you kept the spare key under.

Why all the trouble to project an aura of undoormattishness? Today, Melissa, Zach, and I were going to Planned Parenthood. Or not "going" per se . . . sneaking? Crawling? Slumping?

We'd spent many study halls together over the last couple of days in intense conversation about our options with the pregnancy ordeal. We had run out of options. We had run out of conversation. And I was starting to get this sinking feeling in my stomach that told me we were running out of time. For some reason, none of us had really wanted to go to Planned Parenthood. Especially since it was so far away. But it was our last resort, and, at the very least, they could give us some fresh ideas.

We had to take a thirty-dollar cab ride to Silicon Valley, and Zach and I split the cost. When we finally pulled up to the building, we were all slightly disappointed. I don't know what we were expecting, but this definitely wasn't it. The building was concrete and cold, and one of the windows had a cardboard pane. It was only three stories high, and next to the other buildings in Silicon Valley it didn't look very impressive at all.

Though on the outside it was a very shabby building that looked too unimportant to give us any real help, the inside had been scrubbed up really nice. Standing in the Planned Parenthood lobby was like standing in the middle of a hospital turned therapy center turned school, all done up in pink and blue wallpaper. Excuse me, I felt like saying, but if you're just Planning, then why does it look like she's already had the baby?

A woman walked up to us and said, "How can we help you?"

Melissa didn't say anything. Zach had looked

stricken and vaguely uncomfortable since we'd entered the building. I knew this was my cue.

Me: We need some advice. About pregnancy. My friend Melissa here just found out she's pregnant.

After I said it, the woman smiled, and a kind of relief washed over me.

"My name is Kasey," she said, extending her hand to Melissa and smiling. I glanced at her name tag. It said, "HellomynameisKasey!" She then extended her hand to Zach and me.

"Let me take you to my office, Melissa, where we can talk about your situation. Your friends can sit in the lobby."

Melissa smiled back at me weakly as Kasey ushered her into the office.

I sat. Zach sat. For a while, neither of us said anything.

And then he said: "You know what's strange?"

"No," I said. "What's strange?"

"The way this baby is threatening Melissa's life, and all the trouble she's going through trying to get rid of it, when other people want more than anything to have a baby."

"I guess it's ironic," I said. I was proud of myself for paying attention the day before in English.

"Yeah. Really ironic."

"It makes you feel kind of lucky, actually."

"Did you know that in China there's a law that says you can't have more than one kid?"

"Really?"

"Yeah," he said, nodding, looking rather pleased with himself.

We were quiet a minute more.

"When your mom lost her baby, was she—was she sad?"

Zach nodded and said, "She's still sad."

"Would she ever try to have another baby?" I asked.

Zach thought hard for a moment and then said, "I don't think so. Sometimes the chance of sadness just isn't worth the chance of happiness. If you know what I mean."

"Oh, I don't know," I said, thinking of Tillie. Just then a Planned Parenthood secretary got up from her desk and walked over to us, carrying a basketful of little candies. We both took one.

"But anyway," Zach said, chewing his, "she's got me."

PHOBIA

Jaime: *In every option Kasey listed, you have got to tell your parents.*

MELISSA: *I cannot tell my parents I cannot tell my parents.*

Ten years later . . .

SHEILA: *That girl has got to tell her parents.*

GANDHI

Today I did something that was completely and very undoormattish. I just don't know what got into me. I'd been sitting in front of the TV all night, wondering if it really happened or if I made it all up during some sort of hallucination. But to the best of my knowledge, this is what really happened:

We were sitting in health class, watching a video, like we do just about every Friday. Sometimes our teachers try to force-feed us information about drugs, suicide, AIDS, or other such pleasant topics. But this week the theme was—you guessed it—teen pregnancy. "America's disease."

I have nothing against the video in principle. Yeah, kids should be educated. But not at the expense of another's demonization. But it's okay because I don't think anyone but me caught the way they turned the pregnant girl into a monster. The video on its own was an annoyance, but not enough of one to force me to do anything stupid.

It was when our teacher opened her mouth that I first started having problems.

Unlike the video, Ms. Shelley took her time getting to the real issue of teen pregnancy and started with the "much more pressing" issue of teen sex.

"It's very wrong of kids all over America to be having sex at such young ages, but it's even worse if that wrong act results in a baby." Whatever.

My favorite bit was when she explained to us about how a teen mother had no chance of recovering her life after having that baby.

"After the pregnancy, things by no means get better," she said. "Teen pregnancy often leads to poverty, which can lead to drugs, alcohol, and worse. And instead of one life being affected, two are ruined."

She impressed upon us that in the event that we should find ourselves pregnant (in which case we would be damned to hell forever), we were required to immediately abort the poor creature that we had so sinfully brought into the world.

"You have to understand," she said heatedly, "that

what you have done is *wrong*. But letting a baby exist under the weight of your mistake is even worse."

I glanced over at Melissa, who was sitting cross-legged in the middle of the floor. She was staring at Ms. Shelley as though she were some kind of vengeful angel that might smite her at any moment.

Melissa is one of those very impressionable, easily indoctrinated teenagers whom every advertising agency loves. There's a reason her closet looks like a department store, and there's a reason that between them she and her mother own every diet pill ever manufactured.

The point is that I could practically see all of this taking hold of her. You *must* abort the baby. You are an *evil* person. You should have *no* choice in the matter. You are *required* to drop out of school in order to prevent yourself from influencing your fellow students. You are an *evil* person.

At some point my patience for bullshit just ran out. But there seemed to be so little that I could do about any of it.

It took me a moment or two, but I eventually remembered studying about Gandhi in the seventh grade. Passive resistance, I thought. And right was on my side.

So I took a deep breath, brushed out the wrinkles in my skirt, and left the room. With every step I felt the heat rising to my face and staring eyes locking onto my back.

"Jaime, where are you going?" said Ms. Shelley, startled at having been interrupted by my exit.

I didn't say anything but kept walking, knowing that I'd probably get detention, that I looked really, really pregnant, and that I'd definitely suffer for this later.

I also knew that Melissa saw me go.

When I got outside the classroom, I felt a weight lift from my shoulders. In some strange way the experience had been liberating. One small step for doormats everywhere.

Thank you, Gandhi.

FANTASY

Basically, the pregnancy club has come up with two options for Melissa over the past weekend: she can tell her parents or try to get an illegal abortion.

Obviously it's safest to let her parents know. No doubt about it, spilling the beans is the most reasonable thing she could do. Zach and I have been trying to convince her of that for ages. But when it comes right down to it, the question is, would I?

I would chew my arm off first.

I don't know about my father, but my mother would consider it a personal failure on her part if I were to get pregnant. She would cry forever and wonder,

"What happened to my little girl? What did I do wrong?"

I'm also almost positive that she'd have me abort it.

"Think of your own life," she'd say.

Today I caught myself creating a fantasy world, like I used to do when I was younger. I imagined that something awful had happened to me, and then I imagined what my father would do and say about it. It was idle wondering, mostly, and it's probably way off the mark. The truth is, I can't really remember what my father was like. I can't remember if he used to laugh a lot, like my mom's dad, or if he stayed away from home, like Melissa's. I can remember the big things, of course. Like I remember that he used to call me Jay, and that he and Mom were really happy together, all the time.

I guess that just shows what I know.

UNFOCUSED

Melissa/Beatrice: "Don't think I'm not kicking myself that I didn't finish that real estate course. I should have finished beauty school, too . . ."

I hear Beatrice's voice catch, and somehow I know that Melissa's is catching with it.

On Sunday afternoon I'd seen Melissa at the bus station. I saw it all from our window. I saw her walk down to the street and stare out across the desert like she was looking for something. A minute later the Greyhound drove up to the station. I started to panic then, just watching, but she didn't try to get on it. She just stared until it drove away.

Greg: Cut! Tillie, where was that line?

I've been slowly coming to realize that the sound of Greg's voice no longer gives me sweaty palms. When I talk to him, I sound semicoherent and everything. Actually, with everything on my plate lately, his presence has started to annoy me more than anything else.

I kept a close eye on Melissa all through rehearsal, and by the time it ended, I was feeling slightly sick to my stomach with worry.

INVISIBLE

(MONOLOGUE)

Melissa flirts outrageously with Zach every chance she gets. Yes, she's already pregnant once, but everyone has to have a hobby. It depresses me every time I see it, and sometimes I get angry with her. But then I remember that it's not her fault. Not really, anyway. The fault is mine.

What happened to me that day when I tried to tell her about Zach? Why didn't I say anything when she got confused? Did I swallow a razor blade? Did I choke? Was there a tapeworm clogging my airways?

The answer is no. I was stepped on.

Today I found the Dream Sheet in my wastebasket. I

realized that my health class teacher had forgotten to ask me for it back. It figures. I'm not a particularly troublesome student, and I'm not a particularly good one either. So I guess that sort of negates my existence in the eyes of a school teacher. But I'm used to it.

All my life I've been invisible. Even my name sounds like a name for a nobody. Not like Sheila or Melissa or Guavamatasushi. I decided the year my dad left that if I had to pick one word out of all the words in the world to describe myself with, the word that I would choose was *doormat*.

Ever since, that is the way I've thought about myself. As a doormat.

Maybe I don't like being a doormat. Maybe that's not the word I'd want to choose now. But no one ever gets to choose who they are. The most they can do is try to choose who they become, right? So I think I'll choose that, too. Maybe not right away, but I can sort of ease my way into it . . . like drinking tiny sips of coffee each day until you like it.

Hmmmm. Anything's possible.

The part that bothers me is that Melissa still doesn't know that I like Zach. I didn't tell her when I should have, I haven't told her since, and, let's face it, if I don't do something drastic, I probably never will. I worry about this because it's no way to live. It keeps me up nights.

I also know that for this problem, passive resistance is not the answer.

CHALK

Today I got terribly lost in the catacombs behind the greenroom, all because stupid Ms. Roslin sent me to get more chalk for Greg. She told me she kept the chalk behind the greenroom. Now, everyone knows that no one keeps *anything* worthwhile behind the greenroom because it's dark, and it smells, and it's so easy to get horribly lost. But Greg insisted that he needed the chalk and he needed it soon, so off I went.

It took me easily ten minutes to get to the storage room. It was very dark, and I kept stubbing my toes on things, and I felt like the victim in "The Cask of Amontillado." But I forged ahead, feeling very used and very cranky. When I finally got to the storage room, it took me another ten minutes or so to work the latch open. When I couldn't get it open right away, I started to panic, so I picked up a wrench from the toolbox at my feet, ready to defend myself against vampires, or the Phantom of the Opera, or whatever. When I finally did get the door open, I stumbled around the pitch-black room for a couple of minutes, trying to feel my way toward the chalk. I hit my head on a low beam and shouted in pain.

"What was that?" I heard someone whisper as I was rubbing my head in disgust. The whisper sort of echoed, like it was coming from the other side of the wall. Whoever was speaking was standing onstage. I froze.

"I don't know, probably nothing." The voices were coming from backstage. The second voice was male and sounded very impatient.

"So you wanted to talk to me," he said.

"Yeah. Greg, there's something I've been meaning to tell you for a long time now, but you haven't been answering my notes."

I started so badly that I almost hit my head again. *Greg?* I thought. And the second voice had to be–it had to be *Melissa*! Why was Melissa talking to Greg? I soon found out, to my dismay.

There was silence for a while. I thought I heard someone crying.

"Look," Greg said. "Just tell me what's wrong. I still have things to do tonight."

"I'm—*I'm pregnant,*" said Melissa.

"You're what?"

"I'm pregnant! I found out forever ago, but I haven't had a chance to tell you."

There was more crying. I felt tears welling up in my own eyes. This could mean only one thing. Greg was the father. After all this, I was finding out that Greg was the father!

"Okay, look," he said after a while. "I'm sorry."

I heard a little choke that sounded like there was a smile in it somewhere.

"I knew it," said Melissa. "I knew you'd understand and want to help me."

"Help—"

"I was so worried."

"You want help?" said Greg, and he sounded angry. "If you want help I can get you some money. But I won't if you tell anyone, because no one can know about this."

"What do you mean?"

"I mean no one can know about this baby!"

"I don't—"

"No one I know will ever know about this. Do you understand that?"

I felt a growl rising in my throat.

"So you're not going to help me?" said Melissa between sobs.

"If you want money I can give you money. But this isn't my fault."

Then whose fault is it? I wanted to shout. I had to get out of that closet. I just couldn't listen anymore. I stumbled along the wall and flipped on the light switch, trying to get to the door. As soon as the light came on, I saw that I wasn't alone in the room. Alyssa was staring at me, her eyes wide. I knew without asking that she'd heard everything. We stared at each other for a minute, and then I pushed open the door and ran from the auditorium.

OCEANS

Today is Halloween, my least favorite day of the year. Ever since I've been little I've been having traumatizing Halloween experiences. It seems this one is no exception. Because of the new drama regime, we had a late rehearsal, even today, of all holy days. But that suited me just fine. Doormats aren't into the whole Halloween scene anyway.

I got to rehearsal early because my last period was a study hall. I went backstage to put my stuff down, and I saw Alyssa leaning against the back of a set, looking alternately sad, desperate, and humiliated. I don't think I've ever seen so many complex emotions flickering over someone's face. She was dressed as a purple fairy. She looked cute. What else could possibly matter to her? I walked over to her.

"Hey," I said.

"Hey."

"Can I ask you a question?"

"Sure," she said, running the back of her hand across her eyes wearily.

"What were you doing in the greenroom closet last Friday?"

"Nothing," she said. "I just wanted a place to think."

Think, I thought. I'd heard better lies.

"Okay," I said.

"No, really," she said. "I wasn't smoking or anything. I just have a lot on my mind." Unexpectedly, Alyssa began to cry. I was completely taken off guard. It was like someone spilled dry ice on my doormat or something—I couldn't feel any of my extremities for a while.

Alyssa, crying to me?

"My parents are getting a divorce," she eventually said by way of explanation.

She told me that her dad was probably going to leave the house. Been there, done that, I thought bitterly.

But for some reason I found myself actually sympathizing—rubbing her back, making cooing sounds, the whole kit and kaboodle. And all the while I was thinking, Oh my God! Alyssa crying to me! I hadn't even known that we were members of the same species until today. And what was more, she was crying about this one subject that I could actually understand, that my own eyes had made oceans out of. This one subject that I remembered too well.

"Is it true," she asked me after the wracking sobs had subsided to smooth, slow cheek-stainers, "that Greg got Melissa pregnant?"

"It's true, all right."

"That's awful."

"Yeah."

And you're telling me?

NOVEMBER

Today is the first day of November. We're marking a whole new month. Melissa has made no decisions concerning her life, and time is beginning to run out. The whole Greg thing shook me for a while. I mean, I used to have a serious crush on him, and it took me ten minutes of eavesdropping to find out that he's a total scumbag. But in the long run, he means nothing. It's time to focus on what Melissa needs to do. So I confronted her today. Just to give her a little nudge, you know.

And after this, I've decided, I'm going to stay out of the whole mess. Zach and I think we need to give

Melissa some time to point herself in the right direction, and then we can work things out together again. It's not that I don't want to deal with her problems. It's that I want her to deal with them too. But, like everything else, this is easier said than done. I sat at the breakfast table this morning with a feeling of fear tightening my stomach and airways. I took deep breaths all through my classes. But I wasn't about to let my fear throw me off. We'd wasted enough time waiting around for miracles that aren't going to happen.

(Curtain up.)

ME: *(hands on hips) Melissa! We need to talk!*
MELISSA: *(batting eyelids innocently) Yes?*
ME: *It is time for you to tell your parents.*
MELISSA: *What? I can't–*
ME: *Look, Zach and I have been doing some reading. And your chances don't look good for an abortion.*
MELISSA: *Excuse me?*
ME: *You can't seriously believe that any upstanding doctor would perform a major operation on a teenage girl without her parents' signature?*
MELISSA: *We could forge–*
ME: *Are you insane? Sorry, don't answer that. Melissa! How can you even suggest forging a signature for an operation you don't even want to have?*
MELISSA: *(defensively) What do you mean?*

ME: *You told me you would rather keep the baby. You told me you didn't want to get rid of it. That you would feel guilty. That's what you told me.*

MELISSA: *I–*

ME: *(in a whisper) I think, Melissa, it is time to tell your parents. Before you start to show.*

MELISSA: *I can't!*

ME: *Then I can't help you. You have to make a choice.*

(Curtain falls.)

VERDICT

Tomorrow is Thanksgiving, and as of last period, I have a lot to be thankful for. My worries about Melissa and her baby have been slowly escalating with the passing of time, as has my increased awareness of teen pregnancy news coverage (a favorite topic for the media) and the differing opinions and advice. On one side there's Planned Parenthood, on the other our health class teacher, and on yet another, the people who stand *outside* Planned Parenthood with signs.

The young teenage body is not made to carry the weight of a pregnancy. The young teenage mind is not made to carry the weight of an abortion. To keep her parents' awareness minimal to none, Melissa would be forced to choose an abortion done illegally by a doctor with iffy credentials. Both Zach and I have been screaming *No*! And then we stopped screaming anything and waited for her to make her own decision.

It took her nearly a month, but today the verdict came in.

"Jaime, after thinking about this for a long time, I've decided to have the baby."

Translation—Now that I've finished acting like a baby, I've decided to talk about having one of my own.

"And I've decided that I need to tell my parents."

Thank you, God.

After school, I was so happy that I ran around the soccer field twice . . . forgetting for a moment that doormats hate to run.

RABBIT

Dramatic things have been happening to Melissa all year, but ever since she decided to tell her parents about the pregnancy, I've felt that drama starting to die away. For one reason or another, I feel secure for the first time in months. I feel like her destiny is under control, and I feel like we've done the right thing.

The moment her drama started slipping out of my life, I had room for some of my own.

My drama happened because of this rabbit. The rabbit died today. It wasn't any rabbit I know; it wasn't even a real rabbit. There's a scene in the play where a rabbit dies—and Greg made us play it again and again and again. I was crying inside after the third run-through, and Alyssa had to ask for a break. Even Melissa looked shaken.

Me/Tillie: "Mother, you didn't kill it, did you?"

That's when the gamma ray struck me. Right after those words. Those words gave me a wonderful idea.

With tears still on my cheeks, I felt my heart start to swell. I felt elated. I felt like something had picked my feet up.

After rehearsal, I met Zach outside. Or actually *met* is the wrong word. I stormed him. I stampeded him.

"Zach! You won't believe it! I had the best idea!"

If he'd been Melissa, he would have shrugged it off, turned away. But that's why I didn't tell Melissa. I'd thought about it but decided that Zach was the one who had to know.

"Really?" he said, confused but open to listening.

"Yeah. I'm going to be a playwright. Starting today."

He was quiet for a second, and his silence made me nervous. I bit a fingernail anxiously.

"Starting today you want to be a playwright or starting today you're writing plays?" he said. I stopped mid-answer to that and tried to get a closer look at him, because I swear he sounded just like Sheila at that moment. And then I had to really think about my answer, think about it for a long time . . . was I going to wait until later or do something starting now?

Melissa/Beatrice: "I should have finished beauty school, too."

"Starting today I'm writing plays."

"Great," he said, and turned to go. I felt a great sense of relief when he said that, because I felt that my idea was secure. Now that someone knew about it, it was like it became more real.

"Oh, Zach," I said, spur of the moment, as he was walking away. "Do you like Melissa?" I tried to bite my tongue, but it was too late. I scrunched my toes up in balls in my shoes and hoped for the best.

"No," he said. No? "I mean, of course not."

Semiawkward silence. I've had a lot of experience with those.

"So, um, Jaime," he said. "Do you like Greg?"

Surprised, I answered, "No." And then–"I mean, of course not."

I have a feeling we both walked away smiling.

Translation (of scene)–I think he likes me.

●

Disclaimer: If you're at all cynical about my description of that encounter, and were rude enough to say anything about it, then I'm sorry, but I couldn't hear you . . .

There was sunshine in my ears.

FAMILY

When I got home, I wrote. I wanted desperately to tell someone about my revelation—I wanted to be a playwright!—but there was no one to tell except Jake. And he just blinks at me. If my father were here, I would have told him, for certain. But he isn't. So I told my mother:

"That's nice, sweetie," she said, and went back to filing our taxes.

Since that was not exactly what I was looking for, I pressed the issue a bit.

"No, really," I said. "I want to be a playwright when I grow up. I really want to do it." Talk about a speech.

"Okay, honey, you should, you know, practice."

PRACTICE!?! "Never mind, Mom. Next time I won't tell you about it."

She looked up at me, and her eyes weren't angry, like I expected them to be, but they were sad.

"What—" she started, but I was already gone.

Alyssa called me tonight. I know we're trespassing on all sorts of social boundaries and that I at least should have more sense than to promote this, but I was happy she called anyway. We talked for a long time by my mother's standards, and, heck, even by mine. I swear, behind all the "like, totallys" in her speech pattern, Alyssa is a misunderstood genius.

"You're cool, Jaime," she said, like she was surprised.

"Um . . ."

"Sorry, I mean, I've just never really thought of you as a . . ."

"Person?"

"No, I mean—"

"That's okay. I never really thought of you as a person either."

"Oh. Okay. Bye, Jaime."

"Bye."

Alyssa's plan was so simple it made my ears hurt. But I was all for it. So, it turned out, was Sheila, when I called her.

"It's a lovely idea, sweetheart," Sheila said to me. "I'll make it happen." When Sheila says "I'll make it happen," you can be certain that it will.

After play practice the next day, we put the plan into action. Or, excuse me, Alyssa and Sheila put the plan into action.

A month ago, I wouldn't have missed this day for the world. I mean, it was Melissa's big break. Actually, doormat that I am, I probably wouldn't be missing this day for the world if Sheila hadn't told me to. "Honey," she said, "we have to look to our priorities."

Yes, ma'am.

I had a date with Zach. Cross my heart, hope to die, stick a needle . . . I really hate that saying.

"Good luck, Alyssa," I said before I left. "I think this is the nicest thing we've ever done for her."

"Probably. I'll tell her to call you afterward. Good luck." Alyssa winked at me and giggled.

"Let's get moving, Alyss!" Sheila shouted from her convertible. It's a different color today, I noticed. She likes to paint her convertible every month or so. On the way out, I mentioned that I preferred the silver.

STRAWBERRY

I don't actually like hamburgers, but today I would have chosen them for my last meal. I had two or three, Zach had four or five, and we each had a strawberry milk shake. It's our favorite flavor.

I told Zach about what we had done for Melissa, and he smiled at me. He talked about the lighting and sound for the play and asked me how my own play was going. I told him it was okay. Except I didn't really know what to write about.

"Let's see," he said. "You could write about a city."

"A city?"

"Like Los Angeles."

"Why would I write about Los Angeles?"

"Haven't you ever wanted to live there? I mean, we're all the way out here in the boonies, but in L.A. . . . Yeah, you should definitely write about Los Angeles. You could write about someone moving to Los Angeles."

"Someone without a plan."

"Without any money."

"But with a lot of dreams."

You don't have to say it, because we already know— we're both artistic geniuses.

The date was different than I expected it to be. I imagined lampposts and cool pavements and fedoras and a trench coat. What I got was more like Easter— bloated on chocolate, sunshine, and happiness, so full I couldn't even move. I was so full of sunshine I was spilling over, I swear. I was one happy doormat.

Except, Zach didn't make me feel like a doormat. He made me feel like a starlet—moving to L.A., probably, to conquer the silver screen. People were sending me rose bouquets in my head and applauding me in black and white. Maybe I'm getting carried away. But then again, maybe I'm not.

Oh, yeah, and I got my first kiss that day. Second, if you want to get technical. Okay, third. But let's start the record over, just for kicks.

It tasted like French fries and onions.

SMILE

Wednesday night I apologized to my mom for being
a brat all that week. Ever since the playwriting episode,
I had refused to do the dishes or clean my room or anything. I mean, I was *mean,* and since a week is about the
extent of my anger attention span (Greg being the exception to the rule, of course), I finally made it up to
her. We went out to eat.

It was really weird. She got me French fries, and a
Coke, and she had some dinky salad—but except for the
dinky salad bit (Mom used to be a meat eater), it was exactly what life used to be like. We used to talk like we
were friends or something, like each of us actually cared

what the other person thought of our life. Well, we didn't quite reach that glory, but it was a start.

And better, Melissa called me about the day we'd arranged for her:

MELISSA: *Oh–my–God–Jaime! It was amazing . . . I mean, amazing! They did my hair in these curls and makeup from the juniors' collection (it was a little more natural than I would have done, but still!) and they powdered my face and dressed me up like it was for prom . . . the dress was so* silky and wonderful! *And then they took about a dozen pictures from all sides of me, and told me to smile a little more, a little less, to raise my eyebrow, lower it, and afterward the director took me out to lunch at the Nordstrom café. . . .*

ME: *Wow . . .*

MELISSA: *He said I did great! And he said he wanted me back sometime, except–*

ME: *Melissa, you still have two months to model for Nordstrom before you show. And then you can take a leave.*

MELISSA: *Yeah . . . Thank you thank you thank you thank you thank you, Jaime! And Alyssa was there too, did you know, and she was acting all nice . . .*

ME: *She's great once you get to know–*

MELISSA: *And they painted my nails for me too, like a free manicure, and bought me this great color. . . .*

ME: *Melissa, I'm glad you liked it. We thought it was the least we could do.*

MELISSA: *And there was this guy there, a male model, I guess, and he was sooooooo cute, you would have loved him. . . .*

ME: *Actually I'm sort of taken.*
MELISSA: *What?*
ME: *(smile smile smile smile smile smile smile)*

And then I told her everything about Zach.

DRAFT

Street of L.A.; it's dark and very cold. Starlet is dressed in furs, waiting for a cab at the side of the street. She has a glow on her face, like she's finally finding something remarkable. You can see it in her eyes—she's bound for Hollywood.

CABDRIVER: *Need a cab, lady?*
STARLET: *Yes* . . .
CABDRIVER: *Where to?*
STARLET: *Hollywood.*
CABDRIVER: *(with a funny look in his eye) Hollywood it is.*

They drive off into the distance, and the cabdriver appears by a lamppost, smoking.

CABDRIVER: *I've seen it before. They want to act. They want to shine. But I've never seen one make it. I think it's because there's just too many stars in the world. But every now and then I meet someone with something real. It may be talent, it may be desire, but whatever it is, I can't leave them in Hollywood . . . I take them somewhere else.*

Lights fade, and Starlet gets out of the cab. The lights escalate dramatically now, making a switch from day to night. Everything is in black and white.

STARLET: *Where is this?*
STREET MAN: *Welcome to Hollywood!*
STARLET: *But . . . this isn't Hollywood! There's no color!*
STREET MAN: *This is the real Hollywood.*
STARLET: *Taxi!*
STREET MAN: *No, wait! Stay! You don't want to go back.*
STARLET: *Yes, I do.*
STREET MAN: *No, you don't. Because in the real Hollywood you'll have to hole up in some overpriced stinky apartment with bugs and show up for audition after audition after audition and get rejection after rejection after rejection. You'll watch your dreams trickle away. . . . But here, a director could show up on your doorstep at any time. In fact, he will! You'll be a star.*
STARLET: *But it's not real.*
STREET MAN: *It depends on what you mean by* real.

Zach said I'm going to win the Pulitzer Prize one day. My doormattish self blushed and said, "Don't be silly."

My Hollywood one said, "Duh," and flipped her hair.

Zach loved it, anyway.

Becoming undoormattish is like going on a diet plan. They're hard to follow, but if you have the willpower and a treadmill, they turn out to be worth it. I'm counting calories like a miser counts pennies, and I'm counting them often. Except unlike calories, I want as many acts of undoormattishness as I can get my hands on. Playwrights for $500, please.

DAD

Melissa told her parents.

She came over to my house afterward, and we watched a movie and drank hot chocolate.

It seems that telling her parents was the most painful thing about the pregnancy, and now that it's over, she feels better.

Now that it's over.

Her mom screamed at her about care and responsibility for a while, while her dad buried his head in his hands. After that, her mom began to get kind of excited–"We're going to have a baby," she said, and when she said it she smiled.

Her father barely said anything at all. He patted Melissa's back, and looked disappointed, and opened a can of beer. Later that evening, he went to the hospital to work some overtime.

I have a feeling that my father would have said something, *anything*. Maybe he would have yelled, but I think he would at least have cared.

It was this thought that led me to do the most un-doormattish thing of my life. I looked him up in the phone book.

I almost called Melissa. I almost called Sheila. I almost called Zach. But I knew this was something I wanted to do by myself.

There were four Charles Lemonts in the phone book. I started from the bottom and worked my way up.

Take 1:
ME: *Dad?*
CHARLES LEMONT #4: *Chelsea?*
ME: *Sorry, wrong number.*

Take 2:
ME: *Dad?*
CHARLES LEMONT #3: *I'm sorry, you must have a wrong number.*
ME: *Did you used to be married to a Leslie Charleston?*
CHARLES LEMONT #3: *Who?*

121

Take 3:
ME: *Dad?*
CHARLES LEMONT #2: *Who is this, please?*
ME: *It's Jaime Charleston.*
CHARLES LEMONT #2: *I'm sorry, do I know you?*

Take 4: (here goes)
ME: *Dad?*
CHARLES LEMONT: *Who is this?*
ME: *It's Jaime.*
CHARLES LEMONT: *Jaime who?*
ME: *Jaime Charleston. Why did you leave?*
DAD: *(breathing on the other end of the phone line) Honey, this isn't a good time.*
ME: *Well, nothing ever seems like a good time, does it? I guess you never came to see us because you never found a good time, right? Is that it? Are we not a good time?*
DAD: *Look, Jaime, can I call you back—*
JAIME: *No. Why would you call me back? You haven't called us in years. Where are you? Are you married?*
DAD: *(sighs) No, I'm not married.*
ME: *Do you have cancer?*
DAD: *What?*
ME: *Did you leave to protect us from a life-threatening illness? Did you leave because you're a secret Mafia boss on the run? Did you leave because you work for the CIA and you have top-secret business in Russia?*
DAD: *No, Jaime. Honey, I'm glad you called, but—*
ME: *(with a catch in my throat) Then why did you leave?*

DAD: *Because (I note with pleasure a catch in his voice, too) your mother and I weren't right for each other.*

ME: *Was I not right for you either, Dad? Mr. Lemont?*

DAD: *(Are those sobs?)*

ME: *Dad?*

DAD: *Honey, I'm sorry. Do you need money? (I hated him for saying that. I hated those words. No, I didn't need money. I needed my dad back. I needed someone to mow the lawn with me on Sundays and take me out for ice cream. I needed some- one to talk to about life—someone other than my mom, but just as close to me.)*

ME: *I'm pregnant, Dad. (I spat those words as hard as I could. I don't know why I said them, but I did.)*

DAD: *Oh, Jaime. I'm sorry.*

Click.

Why, why, why, *why* did I tell him I was pregnant?

Any other doormat would have cried herself to sleep that night. Instead I didn't sleep, trying not to cry.

But in the morning I was smiling again at the dress rehearsal for our play, and afterward Zach took me to the In-N-Out Burger, which made me smile more. I told him about my call to my father after our second or-der of fries (I swear to God I'll gain twenty pounds just dating him), and he asked me how I felt about it. I told him I felt like a doormat. A dirty, ugly, scrawny door-mat begging her father to come home . . . I mean, he had a life of his own, didn't he? Maybe he had a new baby Jaime. It was such a doormat thing to do. I never should have called.

"But wait a minute. I think calling your dad was the least doormat thing I've ever heard of."

"What?"

"I mean, I don't think I could have done it."

"Seriously?"

"Yeah. And you did it beautifully, too. Slapped him with a piece of the old days."

"But he hung up on me."

"Oh, well."

"So I'm not a doormat anymore?"

"Being a little bit doormat is good. You're a little bit doormat."

We sat in silence for a while, and I watched in a mirror as an old lady behind us devoured a plate of fries in record time.

"Do you think he'll call me back?" I asked after a moment.

"Yeah, sure," Zach said. Pause. Pause. "Or, actually, I don't, really. But you never know."

"Yeah, I guess you don't."

Who needs dads when you've got friends like this?

"You ready for the play?"

Alyssa called me that evening to ask if I was nervous about the show—we had our final rehearsal that day. "Of course I'm nervous," I said, "aren't you?"

She told me, "Of course, but I know it's going to be okay."

That night after our final rehearsal, I pulled the stupid Dream Sheet out from under my wastebasket. This time it only took me a minute to fill the whole thing out. I thought about keeping it—but you know what? I just don't think I need it anymore.

CONCLUSION

Tillie/Me: "But most important, I suppose, my experiment has made me feel important—every atom in me, in everybody, has come from the sun—from places beyond our dreams. The atoms of our hands, the atoms of our hearts . . ."

(Suddenly the lights are shining in an array of white and yellow, illuminating my hands and my face and making my hair glow. I look to Zach in the lighting box and he gives me a thumbs-up. The lights spin deliriously around my feet, and I feel like I'm moving, even though I'm standing still. I feel like I'm standing in the middle of my own magic Hollywood. The crowd *oohs* in appreciation, staring at me. Only Sheila thinks to look back behind her at Zach, operating the lights.)

"Atom.

"Atom.

"What a beautiful word."

The lights go off, and the audience applauds violently. I smile shyly in the darkness. I vaguely wish that my father were sitting out there, applauding, but I know that the people I have are enough. Sheila, Melissa, Zach, my mom, and me. Jake is sitting in his cage at home, but I know he's sending all his love.

I didn't paint my fingernails red today, because I knew I wouldn't need it. I still have a few strings of doormat stuck in my hair, but everyone sees how I'm different. Even Melissa. Especially Melissa.

The curtain falls, and the noise of the applause dwindles. I wonder vaguely if I can make applause like that for my own plays, but I'm not too worried. How hard can it be?

I turn away from the curtain while Janice and Alyssa take their bows. I'm on my way out.

●

My mom meets me outside the door a few minutes later.

"Honey, you did great," she says.

"Er, thanks, Mom," I answer awkwardly, looking

out at the parking lot filled with other parents congratu-lating their children on their wonderful performance, the lighting, the sets.

"Mom?" I start tentatively. "There's a cast party tonight that I wanted to go to at Alyssa's house . . . and Melissa said she could give me a ride if you're busy."

Inexplicably, my mom's face lights up. "No," she says. "I'll drive you." And she does.

Alyssa's house is only minutes away, and we drive in silence. Mom parks the car two houses away and turns to look at me.

"Honey," she says, "I brought you a present. I was saving it for your birthday, but I thought now might be the best time."

The present is wrapped, and when I open it, I find a thick volume inside. *Great Playwrights of the 20th Century: Collected Works.*

I feel my eyes fill with tears and a knot inside me re-leases. It's wonderful to know that my mother under-stood me, after all, when I told her about my dream.

"Have fun tonight, Jaime," she whispers. "And for God's sake reapply your makeup!"

I give a little start at that, and only minutes later un-derstand why: at that moment, my mother sounded just like Sheila.

BABY

Melissa has finally had her baby. It's a girl and I'm happy about that. She's adorable, with blue eyes like her mother. During the months when Melissa was pregnant I didn't see or hear from her all that much. She left school after the play had ended, and was sent to stay at her grandmother's house in Colorado. I got an e-mail or two from her, and some postcards with lots of snow and mountains on them. She wrote that she was very happy in Colorado and that she was glad to finally be away from her parents. I can't say I blame her for that. While Melissa was at home, her father stayed away, and her mother could barely find the will to speak to her while she sat round and pregnant and doing nothing in their living room.

Melissa always wanted a daughter, and I felt they'd be better suited to each other than Melissa and a boy. A week or so after the baby was born, I received an e-mail from Melissa's mother saying that the baby was perfectly healthy and that Melissa would be returning home shortly.

"Shortly" turned out to be a month and a half later. But when Melissa finally did come home, she was not the Melissa I remembered. She was not quite so pretty, for one thing, and she still hadn't lost all the weight from the pregnancy. Her face was a little drawn, and she seemed to have aged a year for every month that I had. She was also more serene and a little sad. I don't know that these newfound qualities make her any more responsible—certainly not responsible enough for a baby—but I know that it's made her someone completely different from the Melissa I once knew, and in a way that's good news.

Melissa's mother pays me seven dollars per hour to help babysit the new arrival. She tells me she can't thank me enough for helping out, but her face looks pinched while she says it, and she hands me the money like it's dirty and she wants nothing more than to be rid of it. But while Melissa's mother hasn't quite gotten used to the idea that her daughter now has a baby, she seems to love the baby well enough. After all, she always wanted another baby.

Melissa named the baby Rose, after her grandmother.

I will help Melissa whenever I can—she has it hard, really, the media don't exaggerate. But I won't dedicate my life to it, as I might have done a year ago, when her life was in Technicolor and mine was in black and white. No, now I have my own life to worry about too: I have school to finish, a play to write, and a doormat to stow away once and for all.

Lights, camera, action.

If you or any of your friends would like more information about the issues discussed in *Doormat*, please contact

PLANNED PARENTHOOD

1-800-230-PLAN

www.plannedparenthood.org

about
the
author

KELLY McWILLIAMS lives in Arizona, where she shares a room with her semitame cat, Griffin, attends high school, studies aikido, plays piano, and is at work on a second novel.